FOR LUKE MICHAEL WILMER

Bloomsbury Publishing, London, New Delhi, New York and Sydney
First published in Great Britain in 2015 by Bloomsbury Publishing Plc
50 Bedford Square, London, WC1B 3DP

Text & illustrations copyright © Tom Percival 2015
The moral right of the author/illustrator has been asserted

ISBN 978 1 4088 5206 4 (HB)
ISBN 978 1 4088 5208 8 (PB)
ISBN 978 1 4088 5207 1 (eBook)
Printed in China by Leo Paper Products, Heshan, Guangdong

1 3 5 7 9 10 8 6 4 2

www.bloomsbury.com

All papers used by Bloomsbury Publishing are natural, recyclable
products made from wood grown in well-managed forests.
The manufacturing processes conform to the environmental
regulations of the country of origin

BLOOMSBURY is a registered trademark of Bloomsbury Publishing Plc

The day was warm and smelled of summer.
Herman and Henry were busy
planning their holidays.

There were SO MANY
exciting places to go.

But all the BEST places cost SO MUCH money.

Far too much for Herman and Henry.

. . . so he set out to find
a holiday they COULD afford.

Camping Shop

CHEAP
CAMPING TRIPS
PLUS A
FREE
DONKEY RIDE TO
YOUR DESTINATION

A short while later, Herman had everything
they could possibly need for a fun-packed break.

He was SO excited – after all, EVERYBODY loves camping!

Well, maybe not
EVERYbody.

Still, it was all
booked now.

By lunchtime, they had each packed a few
essentials and were ready to go.

As they set off, Herman
felt ready for anything.

Henry, on the other hand, just felt like going home.

Within five minutes of arriving at the campsite, Herman's tent was up and the marshmallows were toasting.

But Henry did NOT find camping quite so easy.

That night, Henry didn't sleep very well.

HOOT!

He just couldn't get comfy. To be perfectly honest,
he was a teeny bit scared.

And that was BEFORE his tent collapsed!

The next morning Herman took Henry into town to buy some postcards.

But they each wrote
VERY different things . . .

Henry TRIED to enjoy his holiday –
but nothing seemed to be working out for him.

Herman got the impression that his friend wasn't having a particularly great time.

So the next day,
Herman didn't just
write one postcard . . .

he wrote LOADS!

Before long, strange packages began to arrive for Herman.

It was all VERY mysterious.

That night, Herman waited until
his friend fell asleep . . .

and he put his plan into action!

By the time the sun rose,
the campsite had been
transformed.

WOW!

Henry couldn't believe

his eyes!

The two friends spent the rest of their time doing ALL the things that make a GREAT holiday.

Everything was just perfect!

But despite everything that he
had built, Herman refused
to abandon his tent.

After all, this WAS a camping holiday.